# LOVE YOU FOREVER

WRITTEN BY ROBERT MUNSCH
ILLUSTRATED BY SHEILA McGRAW

A FIREFLY BOOK

Canadian Cataloguing in Publication Data

Munsch, Robert N., 1945-
  Love you forever

ISBN 0-920668-36-4 (bound). — ISBN 0-920668-37-2 (pbk.)

I. McGraw, Sheila. II. Title.

PS8576.U58L68 1986   jC813'.54   C86-094624-X
PZ7.M86Lo 1986

A FIREFLY BOOK

Published by
Firefly Books Ltd.
250 Sparks Avenue
Willowdale, Ontario, Canada
M2H 2S4


Design: Klaus Uhlig Designgroup Inc.

Printed and bound in Canada

TO SAM AND GILLY

A mother held her new baby and
very slowly rocked him back and forth,
back and forth, back and forth.
And while she held him, she sang:

> I'll love you forever,
> I'll like you for always,
> As long as I'm living
> my baby you'll be.

The baby grew. He grew and he grew and he grew. He grew until he was two years old, and he ran all around the house. He pulled all the books off the shelves. He pulled all the food out of the refrigerator and he took his mother's watch and flushed it down the toilet. Sometimes his mother would say, *"This kid is driving me CRAZY!"*

But at night time, when that two-year-
old was quiet, she opened the door
to his room, crawled across the floor,
looked up over the side of his bed;
and if he was really asleep she picked
him up and rocked him back and forth,
back and forth, back and forth.
While she rocked him she sang:

> I'll love you forever,
> I'll like you for always,
> As long as I'm living
> my baby you'll be.

The little boy grew. He grew and he grew
and he grew. He grew until he was nine
years old. And he never wanted to come
in for dinner, he never wanted to take a bath,
and when grandma visited he always
said bad words. Sometimes his mother
wanted to sell him to the *zoo!*

But at night time, when he was
asleep, the mother quietly opened the
door to his room, crawled across
the floor and looked up over the side of
the bed. If he was really asleep,
she picked up that nine-year-old boy
and rocked him back and forth,
back and forth, back and forth.
And while she rocked him she sang:

> I'll love you forever,
> I'll like you for always,
> As long as I'm living
> my baby you'll be.

The boy grew. He grew and he grew and he grew and he grew. He grew until he was a teenager. He had strange friends and he wore strange clothes and he listened to strange music. Sometimes the mother felt like she was in a *zoo!*

But at night time, when that teenager
was asleep, the mother opened the door
to his room, crawled across the
floor and looked up over the side
of the bed. If he was really asleep she
picked up that great big boy and rocked
him back and forth, back and forth,
back and forth.
While she rocked him she sang:

> I'll love you forever,
> I'll like you for always,
> As long as I'm living
> my baby you'll be.

That teenager grew. He grew and he grew and he grew. He grew until he was a grown-up man. He left home and got a house across town.

But sometimes on dark nights
the mother got into her car and drove
across town.

If all the lights in her son's house
were out, she opened his bedroom
window, crawled across the floor,
and looked up over the side of his bed.
If that great big man was really
asleep she picked him up and rocked
him back and forth, back and forth,
back and forth.
And while she rocked him she sang:

> I'll love you forever,
> I'll like you for always,
> As long as I'm living
> my baby you'll be.

Well, that mother, she got older.
She got older and older and older.
One day she called up her son and said,
"You'd better come see me because
I'm very old and sick."
So her son came to see her.
When he came in the door she tried
to sing the song. She sang:

> I'll love you forever,
> I'll like you for always...

But she couldn't finish because she
was too old and sick.

The son went to his mother.
He picked her up and rocked her
back and forth, back and forth,
back and forth.
And he sang this song:

> I'll love you forever,
> I'll like you for always,
> As long as I'm living
> my Mommy you'll be.

When the son came home
that night, he stood for a long time
at the top of the stairs.

Then he went into the room
where his very new baby daughter
was sleeping. He picked her up in
his arms and very slowly rocked
her back and forth, back and forth,
back and forth.
And while he rocked her he sang:

> I'll love you forever,
> I'll like you for always,
> As long as I'm living
> my baby you'll be.

**Robert Munsch**
is the internationally famous author of more than twenty books,
including *The Paper Bag Princess*. In 1987 he won the
"Vicki Metcalf Award for Children's Literature",
presented by the Canadian Authors Association. He is
also the recipient of the Canadian Booksellers Association
"Ruth Schwartz Award" for best children's book – *Thomas' Snowsuit*.

**Sheila McGraw**
has worked as an illustrator and writer for 25 years. In that
time she has contributed paintings and drawings to magazines,
newspapers and advertising. Her book *Papier-Mâché For Kids*
won a Benjamin Franklin Award.

Both Robert Munsch and Sheila McGraw have children of their own.

Books by Sheila McGraw:
This Old New House • Papier-Mâché Today
Papier-Mâché For Kids • Soft Toys to Sew • Gifts Kids Can Make
I Promise I'll Find You (illustrator) • Dolls Kids Can Make

Books by Robert Munsch:
Something Good • Angela's Airplane • The Fire Station
Pigs • A Promise is a Promise • Moira's Birthday
I Have to Go! • 50 Below Zero • The Boy in the Drawer
Murmel Murmel Murmel • Mud Puddle • The Paper Bag Princess
Mortimer • Thomas' Snowsuit • David's Father • Jonathan Cleaned Up
Millicent and the Wind • The Dark • Where Is Gah-Ning?
Wait and See • Purple, Green and Yellow • Show and Tell
(all published by Annick Press)